The
ALMOST INVISIBLE CASES

by Alice Alfonsi

Illustrated by Rich Harrington

SCHOLASTIC INC.

New York Toronto London Auckland Sydney
Mexico City New Delhi Hong Kong Buenos Aires

ISBN-13: 978-0-545-01585-1
ISBN-10: 0-545-01585-5
Copyright © 2007 by Scholastic Inc.

Design by Kim Sonsky
Illustrated by Rich Harrington
Crime Scene Illustrations by Yancey Labat

12 11 10 9 8 7 6 5 4 3 2 1   7 8 9 10 11 / 0

Printed in the U.S.A.
First printing, June 2007

Table of Contents

Want to Be a CRIME-SCENE

You're in luck! In this book, you'll find three different cases to investigate. Can you solve them all?

CASE #1 — **The Case of the Hidden Hawthorne Jewels:**
Kimberly Hawthorne suspects someone is after her family's legendary lost jewels. Can you help Kimberly find the jewels before a treasure hunter robs her family?

CASE #2 — **The Case of the Perfect Score:**
A boy who was never a very good student aces a test and wins a spot on the *Brainiac Quiz* TV show. Did he cheat? And if he did, who helped him?

CASE #3 — **The Case of the Stolen Skates:**
A talented skater's specially designed ice skates are stolen right out of the locker room in the middle of a competition. Can you figure out who took her skates before it's her turn to perform?

DETECTIVE?

The best thing about these mysteries is that you get to solve them yourself. Here's how:

- **Look for clues:** In each case, you'll find clues that point to suspects and their motives. Read carefully, or you'll miss them!

- **Study the crime scene:** We've provided photos of each crime scene. Study the evidence carefully.

- **Use the invisible ink pen:** Each *U-Solve-It!* book comes with a set of tools that you can use to solve the crime. In this pack, you'll find two invisible ink pens with built-in black light revealers. Use them to reveal a secret message or special clue in one of the crime-scene photos in each case.

When you think you've solved all the cases, check your answers online at **www.scholastic.com/usolveit**. You'll need this password:

LIGHTUP

The Case of the Hidden Hawthorne Jewels

1. Digging for Clues

> HAWTHORNE MANOR
> FRONT DRIVE
> MONDAY, 2:00 P.M

"Aunt Tanzy, what happened to your tulips?" Kimberly Hawthorne asked her great aunt.

The two were driving up the long gravel path to Hawthorne Manor when Kim noticed that tulips had been dug up.

Tanzania Hawthorne parked by the house and walked over to one of the many flowerbeds around Hawthorne Manor. The warm summer breeze rustled her long pink-and-green skirt.

"See," said Kimberly, pointing to the overturned dirt. "Someone dug up the yellow tulips."

Aunt Tanzy sighed. "Must be that dog again."

"You said that the other day," Kimberly noted. "When we found the petunia bed dug up. But I've never seen a dog in any of your neighbors' yards."

"Must be a stray," said Aunt Tanzy. Her jade bracelets clinked together as she scratched her head of silver-gray hair. "It's been happening off and on for a few weeks now. Don't worry about it, dear. Let's just get our groceries into the house. You don't want your rocky road ice cream to melt, do you?"

"No," Kimberly said, shoving her hands into the pockets of her blue jeans. She followed her aunt back to the car's trunk. Then she helped her carry the groceries into the house.

Of course, Hawthorne Manor was more than just an

ordinary house. It was a Queen Anne–style Victorian mansion with a big wrap-around porch. It had dozens of rooms, an old cellar, and a large attic.

For the past week, while Kim's parents were traveling on business, she'd been staying with her great aunt at the manor. Since she'd just turned twelve, Kim thought she might be old enough to stay at home by herself. But her parents nixed that idea.

Kim didn't mind too much. She loved her great aunt. And she loved visiting Hawthorne Manor. It had been in the Hawthorne family for well over one hundred years, and it was full of all sorts of interesting things—antiques, china dolls, and trunks of amazing old gowns.

"Aunt Tanzy?" said Kim, glancing out the kitchen window at the rolling lawn and flowerbeds. "Maybe you should think about getting a fence around your property."

Aunt Tanzy shook her head. "Fencing is very expensive. I'm afraid I can't afford anything like that."

Kimberly was surprised. "But I thought with this big place, and all the stuff inside it—I thought you were rich?"

Aunt Tanzy laughed. "Rich with memories, maybe. No, dear. It's been a long time since I was able to make a good living. I'm afraid I've used up nearly all of my savings by now."

Kim knew that her great aunt was once a very successful artist. She'd had her illustrations published in magazines and books. But for years now, arthritis had made it very difficult for Tanzy Hawthorne to draw and paint.

"Kimberly, I think we've earned ourselves a treat after doing all of this shopping," said Aunt Tanzy. "Let's have some of that ice cream you picked out at the creamery."

Aunt Tanzy dished up bowls of the rocky road. The summer day was warm, so the two ate their ice cream on the manor's big back porch.

"I'll tell you the truth, dear," Kim's great aunt confessed. "I'm about to lose Hawthorne Manor."

"Lose it?" Kim asked. She could see the sadness in her aunt's blue eyes. "I don't understand. Hasn't this house been in the family for generations?"

Aunt Tanzy nodded. "Yes, and that's why I feel so badly about it. When I had some health troubles a few years ago, I had to take a loan out of the bank. This property was the collateral. So if I can't keep up my payments on the loan, the bank will take the property from me. That's why I started to sell off the antiques in the house, just to keep up with the bank payments. But it won't be long now. All of the valuable things will be gone, and the bank will take possession of the mansion, unless . . ."

"Unless what?" Kim asked.

Tanzy sighed. "It's silly, I know . . ."

"What?" Kim prompted.

"Unless the legend is true," Aunt Tanzy whispered.

Kim's eyes widened. "What legend?"

"Come with me," said Kim's great aunt, "and I'll show you."

2. Legend of the Lost Jewels

> HAWTHORNE MANOR
> FRONT PARLOR
> MONDAY, 3:00 P.M.

Kim followed her great aunt to the manor's front parlor. The room had a large fireplace, antique furnishings, and a gallery of framed paintings.

"Kimberly, I'm sure you've noticed these paintings," said Aunt Tanzy, pointing to the framed portraits on the walls around them.

"Sure," said Kim. "They're members of our family, right?"

Aunt Tanzy nodded. "This first one is Dr. Hawthorne," she said, pointing to the painting of a bearded man with gray hair, wearing an old-fashioned three-piece suit. "The doctor lived here from 1890 to around 1935. The next two paintings are his sons. His older son was Daniel. He moved to California."

Kim could see that Daniel was handsome but very serious. He was frowning in his portrait.

"And this is his younger son, Martin," said Aunt Tanzy. "He's the son who inherited Hawthorne Manor."

Kim liked Martin's portrait. He was as handsome as his brother, but he seemed friendlier. He wore a big smile and his blue eyes were twinkling.

"Do you know who this next person is?" Aunt Tanzy said, moving on to the next portrait.

"No," said Kim, looking at the beautiful woman.

"This is Martin's wife, your great, great grandmother, Daisy Chadsworth-Hawthorne."

Kim took a closer look at the woman in the painting. Her blond hair was bobbed in the style of the 1920s, and she wore a red evening gown and a white fur stole. She was also wearing priceless jewelry. A necklace of perfect rubies and rare pearls was draped around her throat. She wore matching earrings and a bracelet, too.

"Wow," said Kim. "My great, great grandmother was really pretty."

"Yes, she was."

"She must have been pretty rich, too," said Kim.

"No. Our family was never poor. But we were never that wealthy, either. There were ups and downs all through the years."

"But look at those rocks!" said Kim, pointing to the portrait. "Rubies and pearls!"

"Your great, great grandmother had many admiring suitors before she got married. They gave her expensive presents, including this set of jewelry."

"Must be worth a fortune," said Kim.

"It was . . . or, I should say, it is. *If* it still is . . ."

"What do you mean, *if*?" Kim's brow wrinkled. "I don't get it."

"There's a story that's been passed down in the family, along with this manor," she explained. "Legend has it that her jewels are lost somewhere in or around Hawthorne Manor."

"Lost?" Kim asked. "How could somebody lose priceless jewels like those?"

"Well, maybe not lost. Maybe *hidden*. But nobody knows. Your great, great grandmother never left a will or any other note explaining where these jewels were. She died suddenly, in a car accident. And when her children inherited the house, they couldn't find the jewels in her jewelry box, her bedroom, or anywhere else they searched."

"Did she sell them? Or give them away?"

"Well," said Aunt Tanzy, "Martin's children thought so. Myself, I *never* thought that was the case."

"Why not?" asked Kim.

"I'll show you."

Aunt Tanzy took Kim up the wide staircase to the

second floor. This floor held the manor's bedrooms and her aunt's workroom.

Kim loved the room where her aunt used to draw and paint her illustrations. It was very large and sunny. And a framed photo of Hawthorne Manor dominated one wall. But the two of them didn't stop there.

Kim's aunt led her to another doorway and up another flight of stairs to the manor's attic. Kim had been up here a few times before. The place was used for storage. It was filled with all sorts of old trunks, boxes, and framed paintings protected by white drop cloths.

Aunt Tanzy approached a battered wooden table. On it sat a gold hatbox. Photo albums were stacked up around it. The words *Beverly Jacobs Studio* were printed on the photo album covers in tiny gold script.

"These are professional photo albums," Aunt Tanzy explained, "from family weddings."

She leafed through one of the albums and showed Kim a picture. The bride and groom were standing on the steps of a church. Their relatives were posed around them. One of the people was Daisy Chadsworth-Hawthorne.

"That's her!" Kim said. Her great, great grandmother was much older in this photo than in her portrait downstairs, but Kim recognized her. "And she's wearing her priceless jewels."

Aunt Tanzy nodded. "Exactly! This photo was taken at a family wedding in 1952, just a few days before her death. And since she's wearing the jewels, that means—"

"That means she probably didn't sell them off after the wedding! Or lose them, or give them away!" said Kim.

"That was also my conclusion, dear."

Kim met her great aunt's eyes. "Then Daisy's jewels really might be somewhere on the property."

Aunt Tanzy nodded. "And if we should find them—"

"You won't have to sell the house!"

"That's right," said Kim's aunt. She pointed to the photograph again. "Just one piece of this set of jewelry would be enough to pay off the bank loan and live on for the rest of my life. Then I could leave this house and the rest of the jewelry to you, Kimberly. Wouldn't that be wonderful?"

3. Repairman Joe

> HAWTHORNE MANOR
> GUEST BEDROOM
> TUESDAY, 8:30 A.M.

Yawning and stretching, Kim got out of bed the next morning and dressed in shorts and a T-shirt. She thought about what her aunt had said the day before. If they found

Daisy's lost jewels, Kim herself would one day be the owner of Hawthorne Manor.

"How cool would it be to have an amazing old house like this?" Kim whispered to herself. "And all I have to do is help Aunt Tanzy find those lost jewels."

It sounded easy, but Kim knew it wouldn't be. A lot of people had already tried to find the jewels and failed. According to her great aunt, the family had looked for the gems in all of the expected places already. They'd searched every drawer and closet. All of the trunks and boxes in the house were emptied, and every inch of the attic was searched, too.

They'd checked the walls for hidden safes, and looked under mattresses, cushions, and rugs. They even checked the old storage cellar, looking inside the wooden bins of sugar, rice, and flour.

Of course, someone else may have secretly found the jewels already," Kim whispered. "Someone like a maid, a cook, or a repairman could have stumbled upon them years ago and taken them.

Kimberly stretched again and went to the window. That's when she noticed it. "The yard!"

She ran out of her bedroom and down the stairs. She found her aunt in the kitchen drinking coffee and reading the newspaper.

"Aunt Tanzy," she cried, "more of the flower beds in the

yard were dug up last night!"

Aunt Tanzy nodded. "I know. Must be that dog again."

Ding-dong!

Kim watched from the hallway as her great aunt answered the door.

"Good morning, Ms. Hawthorne," said a young man with short dark hair and green overalls.

"Good morning to you, Joe."

Joe walked in, whistling a tune and carrying a large metal toolbox with the words *Jefferson Hardware* on the side.

"Thank you for coming again," Aunt Tanzy told the young repairman. "The air conditioner in the front parlor is still acting up, I'm afraid, and I can't afford a new one. Can you check it again? And the refrigerator's a little warm, too."

"Yes, ma'am," said Joe. "I think you might have a leak in both. I'll use my black light to check."

Kim watched the young repairman walk toward the front parlor.

"Who's he?" Kim whispered.

17

"Joe Jefferson. He fixed the kitchen sink a few weeks ago," said Aunt Tanzy. "He tried to fix the front parlor's air conditioner, too, but it didn't take. I'm afraid he's not as good as his father was at fixing things."

"His father used to fix things around here, too?" Kimberly asked.

"That's right. Barney Jefferson used to do all the repairs for Hawthorne Manor—from clogs in the kitchen sink to leaks in the attic roof. Such a nice man. He even took an interest in the paintings and photos around the house. He liked hearing about our family history. Then about a month ago, he started sending his son out here from the hardware store. Probably getting too old and tired to come out himself on house calls anymore. Now how about some pancakes, Kimberly?"

4. Discovery in the Attic

Hawthorne Manor
Attic
Tuesday, 9:30 a.m.

After eating Aunt Tanzy's homemade buttermilk pancakes, Kim went back up to the attic and began to poke around. She couldn't believe Daisy would have hidden her priceless jewels without leaving some sort of note or message about where to find them. And it didn't make sense that she accidentally lost them.

Inside a gold hatbox, Kim found a stack of letters. Under the letters were four small leather-bound books.

"I found Daisy's diaries!" she cried, seeing her great, great grandmother's name on the first page.

Kim pulled an old rocking chair over to the attic window and began skimming through the pages of the diaries. She could tell that Daisy was a woman who loved to have fun.

When Daisy was a young girl, she wrote about some funny pranks she played. She used to hide her older brother's dress shoes underneath the cellar's flour bin. And sometimes at night she'd make ghostly sounds to spook her younger brother.

As she grew older, Daisy went to a lot of parties. She played pranks there, too. Once she tricked a young man and woman who secretly liked each other into going into the same room. Then she locked them inside!

In a later diary, Daisy wrote about meeting and marrying her husband, Martin. Not long afterward, he went to England to fight as a solider in World War II. She wrote in her diary that she was very worried about him. But he returned home safely, and she was very happy. She even started playing pranks again.

According to her diary entries, Martin had brought her a funny gift. It was a special pen he used to write on maps during the war. The pen wrote in an invisible ink that Daisy could see only in the dark when she shined something on it called "the doctor's wood's lamp."

"The doctor's wood's lamp?" Kim repeated to herself. "I wonder what that is."

Kim read some more. According to Daisy's diary, she used the invisible ink pen to mark a few things around the house.

I think Old Daniel looks better with a glow-in-the-dark mustash. Daisy wrote. *It certainly made Martin and the children laugh!*

Kim smiled at the way *moustache* was misspelled. Her great, great, grandmother had made many mistakes like that in her diaries. She was a terrible speller!

"But I wonder who Daniel is," Kim whispered. And then she remembered the portrait in the front parlor. "Aunt Tanzy said Dr. Hawthorne's older son was named Daniel!"

Kim closed the diary and ran downstairs.

5. The Secret Message

HAWTHORNE MANOR
FRONT PARLOR
TUESDAY, 10:30 A.M.

"Aunt Tanzy! Aunt Tanzy! Come here!"

20

"What is it, dear?" Aunt Tanzy stepped out of the kitchen, where Joe the repairman was fixing the refrigerator.

Kim showed Aunt Tanzy the diary she'd been reading. "I think Daisy drew an invisible moustache on Daniel Hawthorne's portrait. Isn't that funny? But we need something called a wood's lamp to see it. What's that?"

Aunt Tanzy smiled. "A wood's lamp is basically just a black light."

"If it's just a black light," said Kim, "then why did Daisy call it 'the doctor's wood's lamp?'"

"Daisy's father-in-law was a doctor." Aunt Tanzy led Kim back into the front parlor and pointed to the portrait of the stern-looking Dr. Hawthorne. "He probably had a wood's lamp in the house to check patients' skin for problems: bacterial or fungal infections, for instance."

"Gross," said Kim.

"They have natural phosphors in them, so they glow in the dark," Aunt Tanzy explained. "That's why other things glow in the dark under a strong black light, too, like your teeth and fingernails, for instance."

"Well, according to Daisy's diary, she used an invisible ink pen from her husband's war service to put a moustache on this portrait. And she was able to see it under the wood's lamp."

Aunt Tanzy nodded. "Okay, let's see."

Kim and her great aunt pulled all the drapes shut in the front room. "Now the room's good and dark. We just need the black light," said Aunt Tanzy.

"Do we have one?" asked Kim.

"As it happens, Joe Jefferson just used his black light to find the leak in the refrigerator's coils."

"How did he do that?" Kim asked.

"He injected a special dye into the coolant pipes," Aunt Tanzy explained. "The black light made the dye glow so he could easily find the leak."

Aunt Tanzy walked back into the kitchen and asked Joe if she could borrow his black light.

"Sure," he said. "What for?"

Aunt Tanzy explained and he laughed. "I'll come with you," he said. "I'd like to see this for myself."

The three of them returned to the dark front parlor. Joe turned on the black light and Kim shouted excitedly. "There it is! The fake moustache! I can see it!"

"You're right!" said Aunt Tanzy.

Kim stepped back

and realized something else was glowing nearby in the dark room. "Look!" she said. "Daisy wrote on another portrait."

"That's her own portrait," said Aunt Tanzy.

Kim, Aunt Tanzy, and Joe all stepped closer to Daisy Chadsworth-Hawthorne's portrait. Joe lifted the black light closer to the painting.

"I can see faint words glowing on the painting, but what do they say?" Aunt Tanzy asked. "I don't have my reading glasses on."

"The words say: 'See *fotograf* that BJ took,'" Kim told her great aunt.

"Why's it say 'fotograf' like that?" asked Joe the repairman, scratching his head.

"Daisy was a terrible speller," Kim explained. "Her diary was full of misspellings. I'm sure she meant *photograph*."

"And I'm sure that's a secret message," said Aunt Tanzy. "Daisy left it on purpose."

"I think she did, too!" said Kim. "She wrote it right on the very portrait where she's wearing her priceless jewels. So maybe it's a clue to remind herself or to let her children know where she kept her jewelry hidden!"

"Exactly!" said Aunt Tanzy.

"You two aren't talking about the lost jewels of Hawthorne Manor, are you?" asked Joe.

"Indeed, we are," said Aunt Tanzy. She walked to the window and pulled the drapes open.

Kim took a closer look at Joe the repairman. "You know about the lost jewels?"

Joe suddenly looked a little uncomfortable. "My father told me about them." He shrugged. "A lot of people around these parts have heard the story of how the jewels are still supposed to be lost somewhere on your property."

"Do you think it's true?" Kim asked.

Joe shrugged again. "Who knows. But I'll tell you one thing. They must be worth a fortune." He shook his head. "And, man, with money like that, a guy could really see the world, get out of this little town."

"Is that what you want to do?" Kim asked.

"Of course," said Joe. "I'm not like my dad. I don't want to run a hardware store for the rest of my life."

"Oh," said Kim. "Well, do you mind if I borrow your black light for a few days?"

"Keep it," said Joe, waving his hand. "We've got dozens of them back at Jefferson Hardware."

"Thanks," said Kim. Joe went back to the kitchen, and Kim turned back to her great aunt. "That was nice of him to give us his black light like that."

"Yes," agreed Aunt Tanzy. But an hour later, after Joe returned to his father's store, Kim heard her great aunt making a tsk-tsking sound.

"What is it?" asked Kim.

"Look at this repair bill. Joe didn't give us his black light.

He *charged* us for a brand new one. And that boy gave it to us used."

Kim frowned. "I guess he's not that nice after all."

6. Marjorie's Visit

The next day, when Kim woke up, her aunt suggested they work in the garden. "More flowers were dug up overnight," she told Kim, "and I think we'd better put things right again."

"Okay," said Kim, even though she wanted to keep searching for more clues to the lost jewels.

The night before, they'd tried to figure out Daisy's secret message: *See fotograf that BJ took.*

Kim brought the diaries down to the kitchen and the two of them combed through years of Daisy's life, looking for any reference to anyone nicknamed "BJ," but they couldn't find a single one.

Now, as Kim looked around the dug-up yard of Hawthorne Manor, something sinister occurred to her. "Aunt Tanzy, do you think maybe someone is digging up the yard on purpose? Looking for the lost jewels?" said Kim.

"After all, you heard what Joe Jefferson said yesterday. A lot of people have heard about the legend."

"I guess it's possible," said Aunt Tanzy. "But I doubt your great, great grandmother would have done something as crazy as bury her priceless jewels outside of a locked house."

"I think we should try to stay up tonight and watch the yard ourselves," said Kim.

"You mean like a stakeout?" asked Aunt Tanzy.

"Exactly!" said Kim. "Someone could be trying to rob you."

"But who do you think we'll catch?"

"What about Joe?" Kim suggested. "Or even his father? They both knew about the lost jewels."

"All right, we'll stay up late tonight. Now, let's get back to replanting our flowers."

An hour later, as the two finished up their gardening work, a plump middle-aged woman drove an expensive-looking convertible up the front walkway.

"Helloooo! Helloooo!" called the woman as she

climbed out of her car. She had short, curly brown hair and wore a pale blue suit with a white scarf that fluttered in the breeze.

"Good morning, Marjorie!" Aunt Tanzy replied with a wave.

"Who's that?" Kim asked.

"Marjorie Wainscott is a friend," said Aunt Tanzy. "She's the one who's helped me hold onto Hawthorne Manor this long."

Aunt Tanzy told Kim that Marjorie was also an antiques agent.

"Marjorie's already fetched me a good price for a number of things in the house," said Aunt Tanzy.

"Shall I take a look at that painting today?" Marjorie asked after the two said hello.

"Yes, of course," said Aunt Tanzy. She led Marjorie up to the attic. Kim tagged along.

"How's business, Marjorie?" Aunt Tanzy asked as they climbed the stairs. "Any better?"

"I'm afraid not," said Marjorie. "It won't be long now before I'll have to give up the storefront in town."

"That's terrible!" said Aunt Tanzy.

"I know," said Marjorie. "But maybe something will come up. You never know when you'll find a hidden treasure!"

When they reached the attic, Aunt Tanzy led them to a corner where a framed painting had been carefully covered with a white cloth. She removed the cloth and Kim could see that the picture was a beautiful, rolling green landscape.

"It's an original Thomlinson," said Aunt Tanzy. "Painted in 1875."

"Yes, yes," said Marjorie. "I remember seeing this when I went through your house's inventory a month ago."

She put on her glasses and looked closely at the painting. Then she asked Kim to pull the shades on the attic windows. Kim did and curiously watched as Marjorie pulled a black light out of her bag and flipped it on.

"What's she doing?" Kim whispered to her aunt.

"Appraisers use black lights to detect forgeries of antiques," Aunt Tanzy explained.

"Sheesh, who knew black lights could be so handy?" Kim said. "I'd never even heard of them before this week, and now everyone seems to have one!"

Marjorie overheard Kimberly and laughed. "Do you want to know how I'm using it?" she asked.

"Sure," said Kim, moving closer.

"Well, take a look," she said, moving the black light over the painting. "Paints used today contain phosphors that will glow under a black light. Older paints don't contain phosphors."

"I don't see anything glowing on the painting," said Kim.

"Neither do I, and that's good evidence that it's authentic," said Marjorie with a smile. "I can get a pretty good price for this, I think."

"Wonderful!" said Aunt Tanzy.

But after Marjorie left, Kim found out that it wasn't so wonderful. Two thousand dollars was a lot of money, but Aunt Tanzy said it wasn't even close to enough to save Hawthorne Manor.

7. Late Night Stakeout

> HAWTHORNE MANOR
> SECOND FLOOR
> WEDNESDAY, 11:00 P.M.

Later that night, Kim and her aunt prepared for their stakeout. They pulled two overstuffed chairs over to an open window on the second floor. Then they turned off all the lights in the house and settled into their lookout perches.

Each of them was armed with a flashlight, and Kim showed her great aunt a big work lamp she'd found in the cellar. "The second we hear somebody digging in the yard, I'll flip on this light and shine it on the grass. It'll work just like a police spotlight. And we'll finally see who's trying to steal the Hawthorne jewels!"

"Okay, Kim," said Aunt Tanzy. "But don't be surprised if your treasure hunter turns out to be covered in fur and pawing for buried bones."

"I don't know," said Kim. "It seems to me we have quite a few suspects now. There's Joe and his father. And there's also Marjorie."

"Marjorie Wainscott?" said Aunt Tanzy.

"Sure," said Kim. "She had a black light, and she's seen the portraits and photos around the house. Maybe she's the one looking for the jewels."

"I'd hate to think so," said Kim's great aunt. "I've trusted her for some time."

"It could be someone else, too," said Kim. "After all, you heard what Joe Jefferson said. A lot of people have heard about the legend of the lost jewels."

"True," said Aunt Tanzy. "But remember, dear, that legend never said anything about buried treasure!"

The pair continued whispering in their lookout chairs until well after midnight. By around two in the morning, however, Aunt Tanzy started dozing off.

Kimberly tried to keep her awake, but it was no use. Her great aunt just didn't have it in her to stay up all night.

"Guess it's up to me," whispered Kim. But after another hour, she was dozing off too.

Soon after, a quiet digging started up in the yard. Kim

was groggy when she heard it, but she forced herself to wake up and listen harder.

Am I really hearing digging? she wondered. It was so quiet, she could hardly tell. She shook her great aunt's arm. "Aunt Tanzy," she whispered. "Wake up."

"Mmmm . . ." the woman mumbled but refused to open her eyes.

Kim wanted to shine her makeshift spotlight on the yard, but the digging was so quiet and the yard was so big and dark, she couldn't tell where the noise was coming from.

Taking a deep breath, she decided to just go for it. She flipped on the spotlight and shined it on one of the flowerbeds.

"There!" she cried.

Kim was sure she saw a pale blue pant leg! She quickly moved the spotlight, but whoever was in the yard had moved the other way. Kim moved the light again, but she couldn't find the digger. Her light kept hitting fat tree trunks and shrubs. Was the person hiding behind them? Kim couldn't tell.

"Darn!" she cried.

She started zigzagging the light around the yard again, but it was no use. Whoever had been digging in Aunt Tanzy's yard had gotten away.

8. An Unwanted Visitor

Hawthorne Manor
Front hall
Thursday, 10:00 a.m.

The next morning, after breakfast, Kimberly was looking through her great, great grandmother's diaries again when she heard an argument at the front door.

"I'm upping my offer, Ms. Hawthorne," said a man's voice.

"I don't care," said Aunt Tanzy. "I'll never sell this house to you, Palmer. And you know why."

"Palmer?" Kim whispered to herself. "Who's Palmer?"

She jumped up from the front parlor's armchair and ran

to the window. She could see a man standing on the porch. He was tall and good-looking, with light brown hair. He wore a golf shirt and checked pants.

"You're being very stubborn for no good reason," the man told Aunt Tanzy. "We used to be friends. Why don't you let me come in and—"

"I'm sorry," said Aunt Tanzy, "but I have some things to do. You'll have to go now."

Aunt Tanzy closed the door and stormed into the front parlor. She went to the window and folded her arms as she watched the man walk away.

"Who was that?" Kim asked.

"Dr. Palmer Pratt," said Aunt Tanzy. "He's a big art collector, and he took a real interest in the portraits around the manor when he moved in next door. But for the last two months, he's been quite obnoxious! He heard about my financial difficulties, and he's been trying to buy this house right out from under me. He doesn't even want Hawthorne Manor. He only wants the land under it to expand his own grounds. And I couldn't bear to see Hawthorne Manor bulldozed for some silly swimming pool or a couple of tennis courts. This home is full of so much history, so many memories. Seeing it pulled down like that would be like a terrible nightmare."

Kim frowned. "Dr. Pratt knows about the lost jewels,

just like everybody else, doesn't he?"

"Yes, of course," said Aunt Tanzy. "I told him all about the house's history when he first came to visit me."

"Then he could be the one digging up the flower beds," Kim noted. "Just like Joe Jefferson and his father and Marjorie Wainscott. Dr. Pratt could have seen clues around the house that you and I are still missing."

"I suppose he could have," said Aunt Tanzy. "But the man's very rich. He doesn't need money."

"It's not money he wants. You said he wants this land to build a pool and tennis courts. If he finds the jewels instead of you, you'll have to give up the house."

"I suppose that's possible," said Aunt Tanzy. "But I hope you're wrong about him."

"Maybe I am," said Kim. "Or maybe it won't matter because we'll find the jewels first." Kim began to pace the floor. "We have one good clue—the glow-in-the-dark message on Daisy's portrait. 'See the fotograf that BJ took.'"

"But where's the photograph? And who is BJ?" asked Aunt Tanzy.

"I read Daisy's diaries again," said Kim, "and I still can't find anything about BJ in there. Maybe we should look somewhere else. What about her letters in the attic?"

"Yes!" Aunt Tanzy clapped her hands. "Let's give it a try!"

8. A Clue Revealed

HAWTHORNE MANOR
ATTIC
THURSDAY, 10:30 A.M.

In the attic, Kim went right to the table with the gold hatbox on it.

As she moved aside the wedding albums to reach for the box, Kim cried out, "The photo albums!"

"What's that, dear?" asked Aunt Tanzy.

"The wedding albums, remember?" she said. "Look at the small gold print on the covers."

Aunt Tanzy slipped on her reading glasses. "Beverly Jacobs Studios," she read.

"See?" asked Kim. "Beverly Jacobs. She must be BJ!"

Aunt Tanzy's eyes widened. "BJ! Of course!"

Kim nodded excitedly. "I'll bet if we shine the black light on these wedding photos, we'll find another message!"

Kim ran downstairs and retrieved the black light that Joe Jefferson had sold them. They darkened the attic and turned on the black light.

For the next twenty minutes they looked at all the wedding photos that Beverly Jacobs took. But they came up with nothing!

"Perhaps there's some other clue within the photos,"

Aunt Tanzy said, tapping her chin. "Maybe we should look at them without the black light."

"Okay," Kim said, but she couldn't help feeling discouraged.

9. A Final Message

Hawthorne Manor
Aunt Tanzy's workroom
Thursday, 12:30 p.m.

Kim helped her great aunt carry the wedding albums down to the second floor. Aunt Tanzy's workroom had the best light in the house. So they sat down at her worktable and began to go through the albums again.

After an hour, they gave up. They just couldn't find any clues to the lost jewels of Hawthorne Manor. Kim drummed her fingers on the table. "Are there any other photos in the house that were taken by Beverly Jacobs?" she asked.

"We'd have to look on the backs of the photos," said Aunt Tanzy. "The studio name would most likely be printed there."

"What about that one?" Kim asked. She pointed to the big framed photograph on the wall that showed Hawthorne Manor and some of its grounds. "We don't need to look at the back. Let's just test it."

After drawing the shades to darken the room, Kim turned on the black light. "Look!" she cried, a moment later. "A message!"

Aunt Tanzy nodded. On the photograph of Hawthorne Manor, the invisible message glowed like a lightening bug under the black light.

"Now I know why our flower beds keep getting dug up," said Aunt Tanzy after she read the message. "Do you think the jewels are gone by now? Did the treasure hunter find them?" Aunt Tanzy looked frightened, but Kim smiled.

"I'm guessing the jewels haven't been found yet," said Kim. "And I think I know where the jewels are. I read Daisy's diaries very closely. The clues were all in there! If I'm guessing right, then the jewels *aren't* under the flowers."

"Then where *are* they?" asked Aunt Tanzy.

Kim grinned excitedly. "Just follow me!"

Can you solve the
Case of the
Hidden Hawthorne Jewels?

Take out one of the special pens that came with your crime scene kit. To read the secret message that Kimberly found, shine the pen's built-in black light revealer on the photo of Hawthorne Manor. What does the message say? Where do you think the priceless jewels are hidden? And who was digging up Aunt Tanzy's flowers, looking for them? Was it Joe Jefferson, Marjorie Wainscott, or Dr. Palmer Pratt? When you think you've cracked this case, check your answer online at **www.scholastic.com/usolveit**. Just bring along this month's password:

LIGHTUP

The Case of the Perfect Score

1. Special Assembly

Truman Middle School
Auditorium
Thursday, 2:40 p.m.

Standing on the auditorium stage, Principal Quintz tapped the microphone. "Okay, kids, settle down. As you know, our school has been given the chance to send a contestant to the *Brainiac Quiz for Kids* television show. And today we're going to announce who that contestant is."

From his seat in the fourth row, Nick Bell elbowed his best friend, Malcolm Dudley. "Get ready," he whispered. "You *own* this, Malcolm, *no doubt*."

Nick put his fist up and Malcolm knocked it for luck.

Both Nick and Malcolm were thirteen now, but they'd been best friends since first grade. Some of their classmates wondered why they'd stayed friends for so long. After all,

Malcolm was a quiet kid, who spent hours at the town library. Nick, on the other hand, was totally out there. He loved shooting off his mouth in the debate and drama clubs.

But Nick and Malcolm were buds for a very good reason. They always watched each other's backs. In fourth grade, when two class bullies started hassling Malcolm, it was Nick who'd loudly stuck up for him. In fifth grade, when Nick was failing math, it was Malcolm who spent hours tutoring him.

Today it was Malcolm who needed some moral support, and Nick wasn't going to let his bud down. "Don't be freaked out about being on TV," Nick whispered. "Remember, you always win when you play at home."

"It would be cool to do the show for real," Malcolm admitted. He started to grin. "But I know I'll be nervous."

"I'll be right there in the first row of the studio audience," Nick promised. "When you get nervous, you can look at me, and. . . hey, man, *look at me—*"

Malcolm glanced over.

Nick crossed his eyes.

Malcolm groaned. "If you do that while I'm on camera, I'll just laugh and flub the question."

"No, you won't," Nick insisted. "You won't flub a thing."

On stage, the principal was finally finishing his remarks. ". . . so let's hear from the teacher who gave you all the tests. Ms. Sullivan, if you please?"

The history teacher took the microphone. "Good afternoon, students. As you know, all six hundred and ten of you took the preliminary exam last week. Then we narrowed the field down to fifty. . ."

Nick hadn't made the final cut. But Malcolm had. He'd taken the final exam in Room 133 last week.

"There were one hundred multiple-choice questions on the final," Ms. Sullivan explained. "And I'm pleased and surprised to tell you that one of our students got every question correct: a perfect score!"

Nick was sure that student was Malcolm. He proudly grinned and elbowed his best friend again.

"Without further ado, I'd like to announce the results," said Ms. Sullivan. "And the winner is . . . *Steven Tate*."

Mystery #1

Mystery #2

Mystery #3

2. The Wrong Winner

Nick stared in total shock. "I don't believe it," he whispered. "Steven Tate's no brainiac, not even close."

Malcolm sat still as a statue. His fingers tightly gripped the cushioned arms of his auditorium seat. Everyone expected Malcolm to win. Now kids were staring at him and whispering.

"Would Steven Tate please come up to the stage?" Ms. Sullivan announced into the microphone.

A thirteen-year-old boy rose and confidently strode down the auditorium aisle. Steven was a good-looking kid with sharp features and dark hair.

Nick couldn't believe Steven had gotten a better score than Malcolm on the *Brainiac Quiz* exam. How could a boy who was a C student at best do better than his straight-A best friend?

"Congratulations," said Ms. Sullivan as Steven Tate marched up the steps of the auditorium stage.

"This totally rocks!" Steven said with a grin. Then he grabbed the mic away from the teacher and waggled his eyebrows. "TV land, here I come!"

Steven's skateboarding friends hooted.

"Uh, thank you, Steven," said Ms. Sullivan, wrestling the mic away from the boy. "Next Friday morning, you'll be excused from school to report to KTXZ's downtown television studio for their taping of the weekly *Brainiac Quiz for Kids* show."

"No class, free at last!" Steven cried.

"The *Brainiac Quiz for Kids* producers recognize the hard work that goes into studying for their qualifying exam," the teacher read off the clipboard. "Because of that, they are awarding Steven one thousand dollars in cash and prizes, just for showing up next Friday. And if Steven is successful," Ms. Sullivan continued to read, "he can win up to twenty thousand dollars in cash, saving bonds, and bonus prizes, including prizes for his school."

The students applauded. Nick politely clapped. Then he glanced at Malcolm. His best friend was trying to keep a brave face, but Nick could tell he was devastated.

This is just wrong, Nick thought, watching Steven continue to shout and pump his fist. Nick didn't know how he'd gotten that perfect score, but he knew in his gut something was messed up about it.

"Before we dismiss you today," Ms. Sullivan continued, "I'd like to recognize the runner up in this contest. If, for any reason, Steven can't appear next week, then this student will be called on to take his place. Malcolm Dudley, where are you?"

"Malcolm," Nick whispered, "that's you, stand up!"

Malcolm managed to rise and wave at the teacher.

"There you are!" Ms. Sullivan cried. "With only two answers wrong, Malcolm scored a ninety-eight. The next best score was eighty-eight. So for all of his hard work preparing for this test, give Malcolm a round of applause!"

Then the teacher dismissed the students, and everyone filed out of the auditorium.

"You should be the one going on that TV quiz show," Nick whispered to Malcolm as they headed out the door. "Not Steven."

But Malcolm sadly shook his head. "It wasn't me who got the perfect score."

"The dude cuts class to go skateboarding!" Nick pointed

out. "He blows off homework on a regular basis!"

"Just forget it," Malcolm advised. "He must have really been motivated to study this time. That's all."

A burst of laughter drew the boys' attention in the hallway. Steven was standing by his locker, talking with his friends.

"Hey, Steven!" Nick loudly called.

Malcolm grabbed Nick's arm. "C'mon, man, don't make a scene."

Steven looked up and saw who was calling him. He narrowed his eyes on Nick, then Malcolm. "What do you two want?" he asked. "To *congratulate* me?"

Malcolm wanted to shrink away. But Nick stood his ground. "What I want to do is ask you a question. Did you actually *study* for the Brainiac exam?"

"Let's just say. . . the answers came to me real easy." Steven glanced at his friends. They laughed and elbowed each other. And that's when Nick knew in his gut exactly how Steven had gotten his perfect score.

3. Suspicious Friendship

TRUMAN MIDDLE SCHOOL
FRONT DRIVE
THURSDAY, 3:05 P.M.

"I'm telling you, he *must* have cheated. . ." Nick quietly

argued with Malcolm as they followed Steven and his friends out of the school building.

"I can't see how," Malcolm countered. "The final exam was well monitored. Ms. Sullivan was in the room, watching all of us take the test. So was Ms. Gold, her teaching assistant."

Nick didn't care what Malcolm said. He believed Steven cheated. He was even expecting to overhear him admit it. That's why he insisted they follow him.

As Steven and his crew gathered near the line of yellow school buses, Nick and Malcolm hid in the crowd nearby. They listened to the guys talk. Unfortunately, the guys didn't say much beyond making weekend plans to play video games. Then Steven waved goodbye to his friends and walked away.

"Come on, let's keep following him," said Nick.

In the parking lot, Nick and Malcolm hid behind a minivan and watched Steven walk up to a red sports car. A young man got out of the car to greet him. He wore a Ridgeville College jacket and his features looked a lot like Steven's. They exchanged words.

"That's Steven's brother," Malcolm told Nick.

Steven's brother checked his watch and glanced at the school's side entrance.

"Looks like he's waiting for someone," said Malcolm.

"But who?" said Nick. "He keeps looking at the side entrance, and that door is for teachers."

Just then, they saw a young woman with short blond hair and glasses exit the building. She wore a plaid skirt, tights, and a yellow sweater. Steven's brother began waving to her.

"Audrey, over here!" he called.

The young woman walked over to the red sports car.

"That's Ms. Gold," said Malcolm.

Audrey Gold was getting a degree in education at nearby Ridgeville College. For school credit this year, she was helping their history teacher three days a week.

Nick and Malcolm watched Ms. Gold from their hiding place. She hugged Steven's brother. He gave her a kiss on the cheek. Then Ms. Gold got into the car's front seat. Steven jumped in the back. His brother got behind the wheel, and they drove away.

"Whoa! Steven Tate's brother is dating Audrey Gold!" Nick cried.

"And Ms. Gold helped Ms. Sullivan give the Brainiac exam!"

"Wait. You're not suggesting—"

"Ms. Gold *must* have been the one to help Steven cheat," Nick said. "She probably did it to make Steven's brother happy."

"Oh, yeah?" said Malcolm, pushing up his glasses. "Where's your proof?"

"You saw it with your own eyes," said Nick. "They all got in the car together."

"That doesn't prove a thing, Nick," said Malcolm.

"But—"

"Listen, there were one hundred questions on that exam. Even if Ms. Gold got Steven the answer key in advance, do you really think Steven was able to keep one hundred multiple choice answers straight in his head?"

Nick frowned. "I guess you're right. But I still think it looks bad."

"Sorry," said Malcolm with a shrug. "But what you *think* doesn't matter. For all we know, Ms. Gold made Steven buckle down and study so he could pass fair and square."

"We need to build a case, then," said Nick. "We need to find some kind of proof that Steven cheated."

4. Discovery in the Dark

TRUMAN MIDDLE SCHOOL
Room 133
Friday, 3:20 p.m.

The next day at school, Nick thought about Steven Tate and how to prove he cheated. He was still thinking about it when the final bell rang.

After classes were over, Nick headed for the auditorium. He was a member of the drama club, and today they were holding their first rehearsal for a new musical called *The Singing Ghosts,* which was set in a haunted theater.

"Stage crew, follow me," the stage manager Ron Ronaldi announced.

Ron led the kids in the stage crew out the auditorium doors and down the hallway to Room 133, the largest classroom on the first floor.

"The actors needed the auditorium stage to rehearse," Ron explained. "So we're in here today. Okay, listen up. The director wants us to test out some special material. If it works out, he'll order more as part of the wardrobe for the ghosts. But first I've got to divide you up into production teams. . ."

Nick was asked be part of the stage lighting team—which was only two people, Nick and the team leader, Janet

Philips. She'd been operating the drama club's stage lights for the past two years.

"Hey, Nick," said Janet, walking up to him. "Don't I usually see you *on* stage? What are you doing *backstage* for this production?"

Nick shrugged. "This one's a musical. And I can't carry a tune in a bucket."

They both laughed. Then Nick helped Janet work out a way to test the ghost material for the director. Together, they went into the drama club's storage room and scrounged up three standing lamps. They carried the lamps into Room 133 and removed the shades.

Janet then led him back to the storeroom and dug up three black light bulbs.

"What are those?" Nick asked.

"They're UV lights," Janet explained.

"What will they do?"

Janet waved for Nick to follow her again. "Help me replace the regular bulbs in the lamps, and you'll see."

They put the black lights in the standing lamps, turned them on, and switched off the overhead lights.

"Cool!" shouted some of the kids.

Nick was impressed, too. The black lights made the white material glow brightly in the dark.

"This'll work great for the ghost costumes," Ron declared at the front of the room. "I'll tell the director."

He turned to Janet and Nick. "That's all for today. You two put away the lamps, and I'll take the costumes."

Janet checked her watch. "Let's hurry, okay?" she told Nick. "I'm supposed to pick up my little sister after her piano lesson."

"You go," said Nick. "I can put this stuff away myself."

"Really? That's a huge help. Thanks!" Janet handed Nick the key to the drama club's storage room.

Nick began to put the lamps away. When he came to get the last one, near the back of the classroom, he noticed something weird. One of the desks seemed to be glowing in the black light. It didn't make any sense to him. *None of the other desks were glowing. So why was this one? Could a desk be haunted?* he wondered, ignoring the slight chill going through him as he stepped closer to investigate. *Man, I hope not . . .*

Finally, Nick saw exactly what was glowing. It wasn't the desk. It was the writing on the surface. Someone had written all over the desk in invisible ink—the kind that glowed under UV light.

Nick crouched lower to read the tiny letters: "adecbaac . . ." He scratched his head. *Say what? Is that another language?*

Just then, in the dark, quiet room, he heard footsteps and knocking.

5. The Disappearing Cheat Sheet

Truman Middle School
Room 133
Friday, 3:45 p.m.

"Nick?" Malcolm called into the darkened room. "You in here?"

Nick sighed with relief and straightened up. For a split second, he thought the footsteps and knocking were coming from a ghost. But it was just Malcolm. He'd stayed after class to talk to the science teacher about an experiment he was working on.

"I'm over here," Nick called. "Come look at this. If anyone can read hieroglyphics, it's you."

"Hieroglyphics?" said Malcolm. "You're joking, right?"

"Just come tell me what this says."

Malcolm pushed up his glasses and examined the desk. "It doesn't say anything. They're just letters."

Nick shook his head. "Last time I saw that many letters, I was looking at the answer key to a multiple-choice test."

The moment Nick said it, both boys froze.

Malcolm's eyes widened. "This is the room where I took the final exam to get on the *Brainiac Quiz* TV show!"

"And the exam was *multiple-choice*!" Nick cried.

Malcolm shook his head. "But there are other classes in

this room, Nick. This could be a cheat sheet for some other test. How can we be sure these are the answers for the Brainiac exam?"

"I'll tell you how," Nick said. "Didn't Ms. Sullivan pass back your test paper already?"

Malcolm nodded excitedly. He rummaged through his backpack and found the paper. Since he'd gotten almost every answer right, it was easy to check his answers against the glowing answers scribbled on the desk.

"Look at this," Nick whispered. "All the letters on the desk are the exact right answers to your test! This is a cheat sheet for the Brainiac final exam—a glow-in-the-dark cheat sheet! Do you remember who sat at this desk?"

Malcolm looked around a moment, and then he remembered. "Steven Tate!" he cried. "Steven sat here. I'm sure of it. I was exactly two seats in front of him."

Nick and Malcolm went to the second floor looking for Ms. Sullivan to tell her what they'd found. But her history classroom was already locked up tight. She was gone for the day.

The boys would have to wait till Monday to talk to the teacher.

6. More Evidence

> Truman Middle School
> Room 133
> Monday, 12:20 p.m.

"They're trying to frame me," Steven angrily argued to Ms. Sullivan on Monday. Everyone was gathered in Room 133—Steven Tate, Malcolm Dudley, Nick Bell, Ms. Sullivan, and even Principal Quintz.

At the start of lunch period, Malcolm and Nick had gone to Ms. Sullivan and told her what they'd accidentally uncovered in Room 133. The teacher quickly gathered everyone together to observe the evidence. Nick brought in the drama club's black light lamp and revealed the glowing letters on the desk.

"But I didn't write those letters on the desk," Steven insisted. "My handwriting doesn't even look like that!"

Ms. Sullivan knew Steven was right. His handwriting didn't look anything like the writing on the desk. She and the principal stepped into the hall to discuss the situation. When they came back, they announced that there wasn't enough evidence to prove Steven cheated.

"We need more evidence, or a confession from a witness," said Nick when he found out the principal's decision. "We need to find out *how* Steven got those multiple-choice answers."

"If he cheated, then Audrey Gold must have helped him," said Malcolm. "But how do we prove it?"

"Let's start by talking to Ms. Gold," said Nick. "We can find out whether she even had access to the test's answer key in the first place."

"Hey, Ms. Gold," Nick called down the second floor hallway a short time later.

The young teaching assistant was stepping out of a second-floor supply closet marked PRIVATE when the boys saw her.

"Oh, hi, Malcolm," Ms. Gold said, quickly closing and locking the closet door. She squinted down at Nick. "And you're. . . Nicholas, right?"

"Nick. . . yeah, um. . . Malcolm and I were having a

disagreement about something," Nick said. "You could probably help us clear it up."

"A disagreement? About what?" Audrey asked.

"Malcolm says all the questions for the *Brainiac Quiz* exam were made up by the entire teaching staff at Truman. But I think Ms. Sullivan made them up all by herself."

Audrey smirked. "Neither of you are right. The producers of the TV quiz show are the ones who made up the questions."

"No way!" said Nick, acting totally surprised. "So how did Ms. Sullivan get them?"

"They were sent over to the school secretary, Mrs. Kim," said Audrey with a shrug. "Mrs. Kim gave them all to Ms. Sullivan."

"Really? How interesting," said Nick. "Then what did Ms. Sullivan do with them?"

"She gave them to me to copy. I put the originals back in the school's master file and gave the copies back to Ms. Sullivan. No big deal." Ms. Gold checked her watch. "Sorry, I have to go."

Nick turned to Malcolm. "Did you hear that? Ms. Gold was the one who made the copies for Ms. Sullivan. She *could* have made an extra copy of the answers and passed them on to Steven!"

"I think we should talk to the school secretary about Ms. Gold," said Malcolm. "She might remember something suspicious about the way Ms. Gold Xeroxed the test answers. If she does, it will help our case."

7. The Envelope, Please

TRUMAN MIDDLE SCHOOL
SCHOOL OFFICE
TUESDAY, 8:40 A.M.

The next morning, Nick and Malcolm got to school well before the first bell. When they walked into the school office, they found the school secretary, Mrs. Kim, working at her computer behind the counter.

Nick stepped up to talk first. "Hi, Mrs. Kim," he called. "We have some quick questions for you."

Mrs. Kim glanced up and nodded. "Just a minute."

She rose from her desk and disappeared through a door marked PRIVATE. A minute later, she reappeared holding a stack of files. She dropped them on her desk and approached the front counter.

"All right, boys, what is it?" she asked.

Malcolm still looked nervous, so Nick continued to take the lead.

"Malcolm would like to see the *Brainiac Quiz* answer key. He's the runner up for the contest, you know? And if Steven Tate can't appear, Malc has to take his place."

"That's right," said Malcolm. "I need to review all the correct answers, just in case. . . ."

Mrs. Kim nodded. "And you cleared this with Ms. Sullivan?" she asked.

Nick froze. He didn't want to lie, but this was an important investigation. "We're sure Ms. Sullivan wants Malcolm to be prepared," he said. And that was true!

"All right," said Mrs. Kim. "I'll just get the paperwork from the file."

They watched Mrs. Kim walk to one of the many file cabinets against the wall and take out a large envelope from the O – S file. She pulled out the answer key page and took it over to the Xerox machine across the room.

"Look," Nick whispered. "If Audrey Gold was going to make extra copies of the answer key, then I doubt Mrs. Kim would have seen her do it."

"You're right," said Malcolm. "The Xerox machine is in

the far corner. Mrs. Kim's desk faces the counter. So her back was probably turned to Ms. Gold. She wouldn't have noticed anything suspicious if Ms. Gold made extra copies."

But before Nick could question Mrs. Kim about Malcolm's teaching assistant, the school secretary spoke up. "Isn't this a wonderful opportunity for Truman Middle School?" she said.

Nick's brow wrinkled. "You mean having one of our students on the quiz show?"

"Of course," said Mrs. Kim, walking back to the front counter. "Steven can win prizes for himself and the school. They give away all sorts of top-quality audiovisual equipment on that show—computers, plasma screen televisions, digital cameras. We can use all of that at Truman."

Mrs. Kim handed over the answer key. "Here you go, Malcolm."

"Thanks." Malcolm took the paper.

"I can understand your wanting to be prepared," she told Malcolm. "But we're all so proud of Steven. I'm sure he'll be able to appear on Friday. I understand some of the television show's quiz questions will be the same ones on the exam he aced. So he should do very well indeed!"

Nick could tell Malcolm was getting upset. He seemed ready to turn and bolt, but Nick put a hand on his friend's shoulder to steady him.

There was something about the way Mrs. Kim had said, "We're all so proud of Steven." She'd said it so enthusiastically—to Nick. It sounded really personal. *Too personal.*

"Do you actually know Steven Tate that well?" Nick asked. "I mean, you seem so happy for him."

"I've known Steven since he was a baby!" said Mrs. Kim. "His family lives on my block, and his mom and dad worked weekends a lot. So they'd leave Steven with me to take care of. He's like one of my own kids."

"Oh, I see," said Nick. "That's great."

Nick elbowed Malcolm. They exchanged suspicious glances. Just then, the office door opened. A man in navy blue overalls walked in. He had good-looking features with brown hair, blue eyes, and a dimple on his chin.

Nick recognized him. He was the school custodian.

"Good morning, Mr. Flax," said Mrs. Kim. "Were you able to have that replacement key made for Ms. Holly?"

"Yeah, yeah," he said.

The custodian walked up to the counter and handed Mrs. Kim a key. "Here you go. If she has any trouble with the lock on Room 222, just let me know and I'll have the key re-cut." Then he turned and left the office.

Mrs. Kim looked down at the boys again. "I'm sure Mr. Flax is very proud of Steven, also."

Nick scratched his head. "Why should he care?"

"Because he's family, of course," said Mrs. Kim. "Mr. Flax is Mrs. Tate's brother."

Nick frowned. "If Mr. Flax is the brother of Steven's mom, then that would mean—"

"The school custodian is Steven's uncle," whispered Malcolm.

"Gotta go!" Nick cried, grabbing Malcolm's arm. "Thanks, Mrs. Kim!"

8. Another Suspect

TRUMAN MIDDLE SCHOOL
FIRST FLOOR HALLWAY
TUESDAY, 9:05 A.M.

Nick and Malcolm followed the school custodian down the first-floor hallway. Mr. Flax unlocked a closet door marked PRIVATE and started pulling cleaning supplies out.

Nick walked up to the man. "Excuse me?"

Mr. Flax turned and looked down at Nick and Malcolm. "What do you two want?"

"My friend and I made a bet with each other," said Nick. "He said you have keys to all the school locks. And I said you didn't."

Mr. Flax jingled the huge ring of keys on his utility belt.

"What does this look like to you?"

Nick shrugged. "A lot of keys."

"I got keys to every lock in this school, kid, even the file cabinets. So if your helpless teacher can't open something, just tell her to call me, okay?"

"I was also wondering—" Nick began. But Mr. Flax cut him off.

"Sorry, kid," said the custodian. "Unless you're wondering how to replace my broken television with a brand new plasma screen, I got no more time to jawbone with you."

BRRRRRRRIIIIIING!

Nick and Malcolm jumped at the sound of the warning bell. It was already time for home room!

"Gotta go," said Nick. "Thanks, Mr. Flax."

As the boys sat in homeroom, Malcolm and Nick barely heard the morning announcements. They were too busy discussing what they'd just uncovered.

"Obviously, Audrey Gold isn't the only one looking suspicious anymore," Nick whispered.

Malcolm nodded. "Mrs. Kim said she thinks of Steven like one of her own kids. She could have slipped him the answer key herself!"

"And Mr. Flax is his uncle," whispered Nick. "Plus he has keys to all the classrooms."

"Well, you just saw Mrs. Kim get a copy of a key from him," Malcolm pointed out. "*She* could have made up a story about Room 133 and gotten Mr. Flax to make her a key. Then she could have snuck into the room and written the answers on that desk."

"Maybe they worked together," Nick suggested. "One thousand dollars in cash and prizes is nothing to sneeze at. Maybe Steven made a deal with one or both of them to split his winnings."

"Or maybe it was just Audrey Gold, working alone," said Malcolm. "She's dating Steven's brother. Maybe he convinced her to help Steven win."

Nick shook his head. "Any one of them could have helped Steven cheat. And that puts us in a very bad position."

"Why?" asked Malcolm.

"Because we have no real evidence against any one of them," said Nick. "So if we accuse *all* of them of helping Steven, it will just make us look desperate."

Malcolm slumped back in his chair. "You're right," he whispered. "We need to narrow our suspects down. Maybe we should try to get writing samples and compare them with the writing on the desk."

"Yeah," said Nick. "But that will take time. And it's already Tuesday morning. The quiz show tapes Friday morning. We'd better start right away."

9. Caught in the Dark

Truman Middle School
First Floor Hallway
Tuesday, 12:30 p.m.

During their free lunch period, Malcolm made up a story to get Ms. Gold to write some history notes for him.

Nick went down to the first floor. He was about to walk into the office and ask Mrs. Kim to write some bogus directions for him when Janet Philips grabbed him.

"Nick!" she cried. "I need your help."

She explained what was wrong as she pulled him down the hall. The drama club just received a shipment of black light bulbs to use for *The Singing Ghosts* musical. But when the box arrived, it was damaged.

"We need to test every light bulb in the box right away," Janet told Nick. "I have to send back any that are broken for replacements. It'll take weeks to get them and that's cutting it really close for the musical's opening night."

"Okay," Nick said, checking his watch. "I can give you fifteen minutes."

He followed Janet back into the drama club storeroom, and they dragged out the three standing lamps they'd used before.

"Where are we doing this?" Nick asked. The drama class was using the stage this period, so they had to work somewhere else.

"Room 133's got a class going on, too," said Janet. "But we can test the lights in this section of the hallway."

There were no windows around them, so they could just turn off the overhead lights to see if the black bulbs were working. Janet plugged in two of the lamps near the auditorium doors.

"We need a third plug," said Nick.

He roamed the hall looking for another plug. When he passed by Steven Tate's locker, Nick stopped and stared in thought.

"Hmmmm. . . " he mumbled. "Steven *claimed* he wasn't the one to write the answers to the exam on his desk. But what if he disguised his handwriting? If he was lying, I might find evidence on his locker."

Nick plugged in the lamp and turned on the black light bulb. He shined it on Steven's locker. To his disappointment, he found no traces of invisible ink.

But he wasn't going to give up. He liked the idea of using the black light to reveal evidence. He just had to keep looking.

He went back to the drama club's storage room and found a super-long extension cord. Then he carried the black light to Room 133. He noticed a glow on the floor outside the room, as if some invisible ink had spilled there. He followed the glowing spots and splatters farther down the first-floor hall until he came to a first-floor door marked PRIVATE.

As he brought the black light closer to the door, his jaw dropped. "Now I know how Steven Tate cheated," he whispered. "And I know who helped him. This evidence is the final proof!"

Can you solve
The Case of the Perfect Score?

Take out one of the invisible ink pens that came with your crime scene kit. To see the clue that Nick found, shine the pen's built-in black light revealer on the photo marked *Truman Middle School Hall Closet*. Based on this crime scene evidence and the clues in the story, how do you think Steven Tate cheated to get his perfect score? And who do you think helped him cheat? When you think you've got it, check your answer online!

Mystery #1

Mystery #2

Mystery #3

The Case of the Stolen Skates

1. Quick Change

> REGIONAL FINALS
> SNOWBIRD ICE ARENA
> LOCKER ROOM, 12:10 P.M.

The atmosphere was electric in the women's locker room. Eighteen young figure skaters were changing costumes, fixing hair, and checking makeup. Their mothers and coaches flitted around them like bees around garden flowers.

As twelve-year-old Mia Ring walked through the craziness, she overheard some of the skaters gossiping about the morning's performances.

"Why was she playing that awful music?"

"What was that jump supposed to be?"

"Did you think that costume actually worked?"

Skate competitions could be really intense. The regional finals were no exception. But today Mia knew the one to beat was her seventeen-year-old sister, Tasha Ring. Tasha had just finished her short program performance with the highest score in the entire morning's first round!

Of course, the finals weren't over yet. The upcoming long program performances would be a big part of the final scoring. And there were still three young women who had a good chance of beating Tasha.

"Your competition looks good," Mia said as she walked up to her sister. "But you're the one who's going to have the biggest *wow* factor out there this afternoon."

"I hope you're right," said Tasha, checking the tightness of her long brown ponytail. She was still wearing her first-round costume—a lilac dress with skates dyed to match. "Did Mom give you the locker key?"

"Yeah, here it is," said Mia.

Tasha took the key and opened her locker. Where is Mom, anyway?"

"She's with the techies in the lighting booth," Mia said. "She wants to make sure your black spotlights are ready for your long program. But I can help. What do you need?"

Tasha grabbed a bottle of water out of her locker, opened it, and took a few swigs. "Start by getting out my special costume, okay? Just drape it over the bench."

"Sure," said Mia. She unzipped the costume out of its garment bag.

Tasha's second-round dress, stockings, and skates had been treated with a special coating of fluorescent dye. During her performance this afternoon, when a black spotlight hit her, Tasha would glow in the dark!

And that wasn't all. When Tasha pressed a button on her wristband, her glow skates would release a thin trail of clear liquid. The liquid was invisible in white light, but under the black UV spot, the liquid would glow brightly.

As Tasha skated out figure eights between jumps and spins, the trail of liquid would show just how precise her skating was.

"Mia, can you help me get out of my skates?" Tasha asked.

"Sure," Mia said.

Tasha sat on the bench, and Mia untied her sister's lilac skates. As she pulled them off and put them in their skate bag, a bubbly voice interrupted

Tasha's quick change.

"Hey, Tasha! What's this I hear about you *glowing* in the dark?"

2. Surprise Appearance

Snowbird Ice Arena
Locker Room, 12:15 p.m.

Tasha turned on the bench and saw Ashley Swan looking elegant in her black dress with pearls sewn all over it. The pearls were peppered through her blond hair, too, which was upswept in a sophisticated style.

Ashley had won the regional finals the year before. So far today, however, she was tied for third. Mia noticed Ashley's mother standing nearby, checking her watch.

"You're not really going to *glow*, like some weird science experiment or something, are you?" Ashley asked.

"It's a special effect," Tasha explained as she slipped her feet into a pair of fleece booties to warm them. Then she reached into her locker and pulled out her specially rigged glow skates to show Ashley.

Just then, Maxine Baxter walked over. Maxine was looking really trendy in a hot-pink spandex dress with glitter. Her black hair was tied into a cute short ponytail.

Maxine had won the regional finals two years before

with the help of her sister Paula Baxter, a former Olympic skater herself. Today, however, Maxine was tied with Ashley for third place.

"My sister heard the buzz about your cool new glow skates," Maxine told Tasha. "Can I see them?"

"Sure," said Tasha, and she began to explain how the glow skates worked.

"Cool!" said newcomer Jasmine Welsh, wandering over in her afternoon costume. Her auburn hair was braided with red bows that matched her red velvet dress.

Even though this was Jasmine's first year at regional finals, she was doing incredibly well. Her high score put her close behind Tasha, in second place.

That's why Jasmine could still win today, just like Maxine and Ashley. All of their scores were very close. Any one of them could hit a homerun during their long programs and pull ahead of Tasha.

And whoever won today would go on to the national finals, where every skater had the chance of making the U.S. Olympic skating team!

"What if the valve in these glow skates sticks or something?" Ashley asked Tasha, studying the skates. "Your glow trail would be all messed up, wouldn't it?"

"Ouch," said Maxine, nodding. "That *could* look messy."

"Your glow line would look more like a glow dotted line," Jasmine joked.

The girls laughed, and Mia's fists clenched. *Tasha's skates had worked perfectly at every practice! These three girls were just trying to shake her sister's confidence. But they couldn't. Tasha had been skating for a long time. She was the coolest competitor these girls would ever meet.*

"My skates work fine," Tasha said with an easy smile. "I'm not worried."

Just then, Coach Dane burst into the locker room. Mrs. Dane was a tall, slender woman with short gray hair. She wore tailored slacks and a blazer and carried a skate bag over her shoulder.

"Salena!" Coach Dane cried, rushing toward Salena Caulfield's locker. "I have some news!"

For years, Mrs. Dane had run a skating school at the Snowbird Arena. Fifteen-year-old Jasmine Welsh was one of her students. So was eighteen-year-old Salena Caulfield.

Salena had skated in the regional finals every year for the past five years, but she'd never won. At the moment, she was in tenth place. So she didn't have much chance of winning today, either.

"The arena's about to make an announcement!" Coach Dane cried. "Ivana Zarkov is here! She's making a surprise appearance! She's going to skate for the crowd!"

The locker room exploded at this news. The girls around Tasha squealed. "Ivana Zarkov! No way!"

Ivana Zarkov was a legend: a five-time Olympic Gold

Medalist in singles figure skating. She hadn't been scheduled to perform. Her appearance was a last-minute surprise to everyone.

Shouts of excitement filled the room. The skaters, their coaches, and their mothers rushed to the locker-room door to see Ivana *live* on the arena ice.

Tasha and Mia ran with the crowd. Racing out into the arena, they left Tasha's special glow skates behind on the locker-room floor.

3. The Disappearing Skates

> SNOWBIRD ICE ARENA
> LOCKER ROOM, 12:30 P.M.

Fifteen minutes later, Ivana Zarkov was taking her bows on the ice. Tasha clapped and clapped, then went back into the empty locker room to finish changing for her long program performance. But when she arrived at her open locker, she stopped and stared in disbelief.

"My special skates!" she cried. "Where are they?"

Mia was right on her sister's heels. "Tasha? What's the matter?"

"My special skates were right here—" She pointed to the carpeting in front of her open locker. "But now they're gone! Where did you put them, Mia?"

75

"What?" Mia cried. "I didn't put them anywhere!"

"Tasha," called Mrs. Ring as she strode into the locker room. "Aren't you changed yet?"

In her youth, Mrs. Ring herself had been a top-ranked figure skater. Now she was her daughter's coach. As Tasha told her the bad news, she wrung her hands.

"Did you misplace the skates?" Mrs. Ring asked.

"No," Tasha told her mom. "I'm sure I left them right here." Once again, she pointed to the carpet in front of her open locker.

Mrs. Ring stood very still for a moment. If they couldn't find Tasha's special glow skates, she'd be forced to wear the lilac skates from her short program. They didn't match her second-round costume, and the special glow effects they'd worked so hard on would be useless!

"Tasha's glow skates have to be here somewhere," murmured Mrs. Ring.

Frantically, Tasha's mother began emptying out locker number three. She took out Tasha's street clothes, her coat, and her snow boots. But Tasha's special ice skates weren't in there. They weren't in their skate bag, either.

Mrs. Ring stepped back and shook her head. She began pulling on the doors of the lockers next to Tasha's, but they were all locked.

"Now what?" whispered Tasha, sounding scared. "I was doing so well with my first-round scores. But if I don't find those skates, I'll be in big trouble!"

"I know, honey." Mrs. Ring checked her watch. "Don't panic, okay? You're the very last one to perform in the afternoon lineup, so we have some time to find them." She put her hands on Tasha's shoulders. "Think, okay? Where could you have put your skates—"

"Look," Mia interrupted.

Tasha turned to see her little sister pointing at a nearby area of the locker-room carpet. "What?" Tasha asked. "Look at what?"

"At this," said Mia, bending down.

Mia noticed something they hadn't. She reached to pick it up and then held it out to them.

"What's that?" Tasha asked.

"It's a pearl," said Mia. "There are tiny white pearls on

the floor by your locker."

Tasha threw up her hands. "So?"

"It's evidence," said Mia.

"Evidence of what?" Tasha asked.

"Evidence of who may have taken your skates," said Mia.

Tasha and Mrs. Ring froze for a moment.

"Mia, do you think someone *took* Tasha's skates?" Mrs. Ring asked.

Mia nodded. "I was in here with Tasha before we all left the locker room. And I remember the skates being right where she said they were. Tasha's skates didn't get up and glide away themselves. They were *stolen*. I'm sure of it."

"But who stole them?" asked Mrs. Ring.

Mia looked around some more. She noticed a red velvet ribbon close by. And she also pointed out some white glitter.

"The pearls, the red ribbon, and the glitter could *all* be evidence," Mia declared.

"Of what?" Tasha asked.

"Let me spell it out for you," said Mia. "Jasmine Welsh is wearing a red velvet dress with matching ribbons for her second-round program."

Mrs. Ring's eyes widened. "Jasmine's score is only a fraction behind Tasha's."

"And these pearls must belong to Ashley Swan," said Mia. "She's wearing black, with pearls like these all over her costume. And Maxine Baxter is wearing a hot-pink spandex dress with white glitter like this."

Mrs. Ring nodded. "Ashley and Maxine are tied for third place, right behind Jasmine. Do you think one of those girls took Tasha's skates? Or maybe all three worked together to sabotage Tasha!"

"I can't believe they would do something like that," said Tasha. "We all worked so hard to get here. None of us would want to win by cheating."

"Don't be so sure," said Mrs. Ring.

"But there's a simple explanation for those things being on the carpet," said Tasha. "All three of those girls came over to my locker just before we ran out of the locker room to see Ivana Zarkov perform."

"What were they doing by your locker, Tasha?" Mrs. Ring asked.

Tasha didn't reply. But Mia spoke right up. "Those girls came over to see Tasha's special glow skates," she told her mother. "They were all curious about them."

Mrs. Ring shook her head. "That sounds like guilty behavior to me, don't you think?" she said.

"Yes, it does," said Mia.

"I'll be right back," said Mrs. Ring. "In the meantime, Tasha, change into your glow dress and stockings. Mia, help your sister."

"But where are you going?" Mia asked.

"To find those three girls," said Mrs. Ring. "I'm going to demand they open up their lockers for me, *right now*."

4. The Disappearing Skates

SNOWBIRD ICE ARENA
LOCKER ROOM, 12:40 P.M.

As the skaters and coaches returned to the locker room and finished primping for the afternoon performances, Mrs. Ring rounded up Jasmine, Ashley, and Maxine. She explained the situation, and all three appeared surprised.

As Mia continued to help her sister change, Tasha's three closest competitors opened their lockers. Mrs. Ring searched each one. But there was no sign of Tasha's special glow skates in lockers three, nine, or twelve.

Mrs. Ring apologized to the girls. But she wasn't giving up. She walked out of the locker room again and brought back Mrs. Gramercy, the Snowbird Arena's manager.

"You have to open every locker in here," Mrs. Ring said, after explaining the situation. "My daughter's skates have to be here somewhere."

"Why?" said the arena manager. "If someone stole them, she would have to know that the lockers are the first place we'd look. She probably snuck them out of here and hid them somewhere else by now."

"I think my mom's right. The skates have to be in a locker," said Mia,

"Why's that?" asked Mrs. Gramercy.

"Because," said Mia with a shrug, "I didn't see a soul come out of or go into the locker room during Ivana Zarkov's entire performance."

"You were watching the door?" the arena manager asked skeptically. "Why weren't you watching Ivana?"

"I was watching Ivana," said Mia. "But I'm a lot shorter than the older girls. So I climbed onto those crates stacked right next to the locker-room door to get a better view of the ice. If someone went in or out that door during Ivana's performance, I would have seen it."

"Then how did my skates get stolen?" Tasha wondered aloud.

"I think I know how," said Mia. "In all the excitement as we were rushing to see Ivana, one of the girls must have grabbed your skates and thrown them into her locker."

"But we already checked the lockers of Jasmine, Ashley, and Maxine," said Tasha. "They're the only skaters who have a chance at beating me. None of the other fourteen girls have strong enough short program scores. So why would any of them risk getting sanctioned for stealing my skates?"

"Beats me," said Mia. "I just think Mom's right. We need

to check every locker."

And that's what they did. The arena manager used her universal key to open every locker in the women's locker room.

"Locker one, Gracie Shine," she said, opening the first locker. "Locker two, Nina Powell . . ."

None of the girls, their coaches, or mothers objected to having Mrs. Gramercy and Mrs. Ring search their lockers. Everyone appeared horrified to hear that someone might have stolen Tasha's special glow skates. And they all wanted to prove their own innocence.

"Locker six, Trixie Jacobs. . . locker seven, Selena Caulfied. . . locker eight, P.J. Smithton. . . locker nine, Ashley Swan. . ."

They continued going through every locker. But once again, Tasha's skates were nowhere to be found.

5. One More Look

By now, the midday break was over and the long program performances were underway. Tasha didn't have a lot of time left to find her skates.

"Tasha," said Mrs. Ring, "I'm afraid we have to face it. We can't do your special glow effects. Take off your fleece booties and put on your lilac skates."

"But they won't match my dress for the long program!" cried Tasha, with tears in her eyes.

"It'll be okay," she told Tasha. "Just skate your very best out there, honey."

Mia gritted her teeth. Her sister didn't deserve this. As her mother helped her sister get ready, Mia began to pace and think.

"Those glow skates have to be somewhere," she whispered to herself. "I found evidence once. Maybe I will again."

By now, the locker room was nearly empty. A few skaters and coaches were still here. But most were in the arena, watching the other girls perform on the ice.

Mia began to walk through the locker room. She trained

her eyes on the carpet, looking for evidence of something, *anything*.

The locker room was pretty clean. Its carpet was vacuumed every night, so she didn't see much dirt. She noticed a few empty water bottles, some tissues, and loose hairpins. None of those things were helpful clues, so she made her way back to her sister's locker—locker number three.

"Mia, we're going out to the arena floor to watch the other skaters," said Mrs. Ring. Tasha was already heading for the door.

"Okay," said Mia. "I'll be along in a minute."

After her mother and sister left, Mia sat down on the padded bench. She closed her eyes and tried to remember exactly what had happened before the skates went missing.

"The glow skates were right here," she mumbled to herself, opening her eyes to stare at the spot of empty carpet.

"Tasha was showing the skates to Ashley, Maxine, and Jasmine . . . and then we heard about Ivana Zarkov's surprise appearance. Tasha put the skates down and we ran out . . ."

Mia pretended to put the skates down. She got up and reenacted her walk toward the locker-room door.

"There were still people in the locker room behind us,"

she realized, "but they were all rushing out, too. Everyone was out the door in a matter of maybe thirty seconds . . ."

Mia turned around and looked at the locker room. "But thirty seconds would have been enough time for someone to run over to Tasha's locker . . ."

Mia paced back and forth in thought. *If I were stealing Tasha's skates, I would have picked them up . . . and then what? I couldn't walk out with them, or someone might see me taking them. But I could have quickly grabbed the skates and thrown them into a locker. We searched all the lockers, but it took awhile to get Mrs. Gramercy here. Someone could have snuck the skates out again.*

Mia ran back to her sister's locker and pretended to reenact grabbing the skates. As she bent all the way down, she noticed a tiny square of green in the carpet underneath the bench.

"Hello!" she cried.

Mia reached for the green square and pulled it up. She saw it was a small sticker with the letters 'SG' printed on it.

"Where have I seen this before?" she wondered. And then she remembered. She looked down at the Snowbird Arena floor access badge pinned on her sweater. "SG stands for Special Guest!"

Everyone in each skater's entourage—her coach, her mother, or anyone helping her on the main floor—received a special access badge with that same green square sticker.

The SG sticker was still stuck to Mia's badge. "So where did this one come from?" she murmured.

Mia ran out of the locker room. She found her mom on the arena floor. "Can I see your floor access badge?" she asked.

The green square sticker was still on her mom's badge. *That meant the sticker she'd found belonged to someone else!*

"Mom, look what I found under the bench in front of Tasha's locker." Mia showed her mom the green SG sticker. "The locker room's carpet is vacuumed every night, so this sticker must have been dropped today."

"But who dropped it?" asked Mrs. Ring.

"I don't know," said Mia. "But if we find out, I'll bet we'll find the person who took Tasha's glow skates!"

6. Not So Clueless

SNOWBIRD ICE ARENA
MAIN FLOOR, 1:15 P.M.

Mrs. Ring was skeptical about Mia's theory. "Remember, Mia, you found pearls, a ribbon, and some glitter on the carpet, too. But that evidence didn't get us anywhere. Tasha's skates weren't in Ashley's, Maxine's, or Jasmine's lockers. Haven't you ever heard the term 'crying wolf'?"

"Okay, Mom," Mia said. "I'll chill. Don't worry."

But Mia couldn't chill. Her mind kept working on the mystery. She glanced around the main floor. This area of benches, right next to the arena ice, was reserved for the competitors and their entourages.

By now, Ashley Swan had already performed. Her scores were very high—high enough to win if Tasha messed up her long program.

Mia narrowed her eyes at Ashley and her mother, a petite woman with curly blond hair. *Could Ashley's mom have stolen Tasha's skates? Maybe.*

Mia *had* to see whether the woman's badge still had its green SG sticker on it. Slipping out of her seat, she walked over to Ashley and her mother. At twelve, Mia just hoped she was young enough to act clueless and get away with snooping!

"Hi, Ashley," she said brightly.

Ashley's mom narrowed her eyes at Mia. For a second, she seemed annoyed. "This area is restricted, little girl—" Mrs.

Swan began to say.

"It's okay, Mom," Ashley said. She looked down at Mia. "You're Tasha's little sister, right?"

"Right," said Mia with a smile. "I just wanted to say that your long program was awesome."

Ashley immediately preened. "Thanks. I hope your sister does okay, too. I mean . . . we all heard about her missing skates. It's a shame."

Mia shrugged. "She'll be fine. I'm sure she'll win."

"No offense," said Ashley. "But I won last year. So it's only right that I win again."

"You deserve to, dear," said Ashley's mom. "This is the year that counts."

Mia scratched her head, pretending to be clueless. "Why does this year count more than last year?"

Ashley's mother frowned with impatience. "Because this is the year my Ashley can qualify for the Olympic team, of course! So it's only fair she should win again this year. Now run along, little girl."

Mia tried to lean closer, to see Mrs. Swan's badge. But she was wearing it backward on her shoelace necklace. Mia couldn't see the front. And she couldn't tell if the green SG sticker was missing.

Mia tried to think up some stupid reason to want to see the front of Mrs. Swan's badge, but it was too late. Both

Ashley and her mother were already turning away and heading quickly for the locker room.

Mia sighed and looked around. On the ice, Salena Caulfield was performing her long program. She wasn't doing very well. There were some wobbles on her spins and awkward lands on her jumps.

Then Mia noticed Maxine Baxter. She was hanging out nearby. Standing beside her was a slender, African-American woman in her thirties. The woman wore a hot pink tracksuit to match Maxine's pink, glittery costume.

Guess it's time to check out Maxine's special guest, Mia decided.

7. Snooping Sister

> SNOWBIRD ICE ARENA
> MAIN FLOOR, 1:30 P.M.

Paula Baxter had once been a great skater. Years ago, she'd made the Olympic team. But during a performance, she'd injured her knee and was never able to skate at world-class level again. That's why she wanted her younger sister, Maxine, to win today.

"I came home from Europe without one medal," Paula was reminding her little sister as Mia snuck up on them. "But you're going to make up for my loss. You're going to win the Gold. I'm sure of it."

"Well, first I've got to win today," Maxine reminded her.

Paula checked her watch. "You're on in another fifteen minutes. Start doing your stretches, okay?"

Maxine nodded and began to stretch her legs.

"Hi, Maxine!" Mia called, walking up to the two Baxters.

"Uh . . . hi," said Maxine, giving Mia a nod.

"Who's this?" asked Paula, frowning tensely.

"I'm Tasha Ring's little sister," said Mia. "I just wanted to wish Maxine luck."

"Oh," said Paula, relaxing a little.

"Well, you better hurry. I'm her coach, and Maxine needs to stretch. She has to skate soon."

"You're Paula Baxter, aren't you?" asked Mia. "You actually skated in the Olympics once, right?"

Paula laughed. "You must have been a tiny baby when that happened."

"I heard people talking about it," said Mia. "Skaters gossip a lot, you know?"

Paula laughed again, and Maxine rolled her eyes.

"No kidding," said Maxine.

"Anyway, I think that's cool," said Mia. "Good luck to you both."

"Thanks," said Paula. "You're very nice, Mia, but we have to get ready for Maxine's performance. So go back to your family, okay?"

Paula tried to shoo Mia away, but she dug in her heels. "I was just wondering, Ms. Baxter . . . could I see your floor badge for a second—"

"I don't have it around my neck anymore, sweetie," she told Mia. "The string on it broke, so I threw it in Maxine's skate bag. Now get going, I don't have time for your games. I mean it."

Paula turned Mia around and gave her a push. Then she turned back to her sister and began to help her stretch.

Mia walked away, but she remained suspicious. *Was the string really broken on Paula Baxter's badge? Or was she trying to hide the fact that she lost the green SG sticker by Tasha's locker?*

8. Enlightening Clue

The final person Mia wanted to check out was Jasmine Welsh's special guest. But Jasmine didn't appear to have a special guest. She was standing all alone in the restricted area.

"Isn't anyone here with you?" Mia asked, walking up to her.

Jasmine explained that her family was sitting up in the stands. She only had one special guest with her down on the main floor—her coach.

"And who's your coach again?" Mia asked.

"Here she comes," said Jasmine, pointing to a tall woman with short gray hair, wearing tailored slacks and a blazer.

Mia recognized Coach Dane, who was also Salena Caulfield's coach.

"I accompanied Salena back to her locker," Coach Dane said as she walked up to Jasmine. "I could have simply given her back her locker seven key, but she needed a little comfort after her poor score. I'm afraid she'll never be in your league, Jasmine."

"Thanks," said Jasmine. "I just hope I don't let you down

today, Mrs. Dane."

Mia stepped back and let Coach Dane continue to talk. The woman didn't notice Mia hanging around nearby.

"Oh, Jasmine!" said Coach Dane. "Just imagine winning the very first regional finals you ever enter! What a headline that will be in the skating news. It will boost my skating school's reputation a thousand percent!"

"I hope so, Mrs. Dane," said Jasmine. "You've helped me a lot."

"You're a natural, Jasmine," said Coach Dane.

Mia crept closer to the tall woman. She tried to get a look at the badge hanging around her neck. *Was there a green sticker on it? Or not?*

"Oh!" Coach Dane cried, suddenly seeing Mia. "What are you doing there?"

"J-just checking your badge, ma'am," Mia stammered.

"Why?" Coach Dane frowned. "There's nothing wrong with it, is there? I lost the old one. This is a replacement."

"Really?" said Mia, suddenly suspicious. *The green SG sticker was there on the badge. But the woman just admitted the badge was a replacement.*

Had Mrs. Dane gotten a replacement badge because she'd lost the green SG sticker on her old one? Was she the one who dropped the sticker by her sister's locker? Or was it Paula Baxter or Mrs. Swan?

Mia tried to ask more questions of Coach Dane, but once again she got shooed away.

Mia went back to her mother and sister. Tasha was beginning to stretch to pass the time. But it wouldn't be long now. Tasha would be on the ice very soon.

"Mia," called Mrs. Ring, "would you take this gym bag back to the locker room and throw it in Tasha's locker? We have too much stuff out here."

"Sure, Mom," said Mia, taking the locker key and the bag.

After hauling the bag back into the locker room, she set it on the padded bench and unzipped it. Her mother had packed some chewing gum in the bag. Mia began pawing through all the junk to find it. As she searched, the bag slipped and fell.

"Darn!"

A number of items fell out, including a small black light. Mia's mom had used the black light early this morning to test the glow dye in her sister's skates.

As she bent down to pick it up, she realized the black light had accidentally turned on. Now it was shining on the carpet, and Mia noticed something funny. The black light was making a tiny part of the carpet *glow*.

Mia ran to turn off the locker-room lights. She rushed back to her sister's locker and shined the black light again. What it revealed on the carpet made Mia gasp.

"*Omigosh!*" she cried. "Tasha's glow dye! I can see it!"

Whoever had taken Tasha's skates had obviously grabbed the skates by their heels and accidentally opened the valve near the blades.

The glow dye had leaked out and left a glowing trail across the locker-room floor. The dye was designed to evaporate quickly on the ice, but here on the carpet, it was still glowing!

Studying it, Mia realized that her theory had been right all along. The thief had taken Tasha's skates, thrown them into a locker, and snuck them out again while no one was looking.

After following the glow trail, Mia was almost certain she knew who the thief was. "I have to tell my mom," she cried, running out of the locker room. "I think I know who stole Tasha's skates!"

Can you solve
The Case of
the Stolen Skates?

Take out one of the pens that came with your crime scene kit. To see the clue that Mia found, shine the pen's built-in black light revealer on the photo marked *Snowbird Ice Arena Locker Room*. Judging from this crime-scene evidence and the clues in the story, who do you think stole Tasha Ring's special glow skates? Was it Mrs. Swan, Paula Baxter, or Coach Dane? When you've got the answer, check out the *U-Solve-It!* web site to see if you're right!